# Anna's Amazing Alaskan Adventure

Mark McCraw

The story, all names, characters, and incidents portrayed in this production are fictitious. No identification with actual persons (living or deceased), places, buildings, or products is intended or should be inferred.

ISBN:  979-8-218-70093-5

Formatted and Illustrated by Iris Davydenko

Cover Image: Iris Davydenko

This book is dedicated to all
amazing children with an
adventurous spirit.

# Chapter 1:
# INTRODUCTION

My name is Anna. I am eleven years old and about five foot seven inches tall with long brown hair and blue eyes. I live in Abbeville, Oklahoma, on one acre of land with an amazing four-bedroom, two-story house and a barn across from a pond. We have alpacas and armadillos on our farm. There are also alligator gars in the pond. Sometimes, I see antelopes near my house. We even have an African parrot in our house.

Grandpa Alvin, an accountant and former architect, is taking me on an Alaskan cruise on the All-American Cruise Line during August. Grandpa Alvin showed me the advertisement from the travel agency. I was simply amazed at the adventurous-looking brochure that the travel agent gave him.

Because it was his tenth anniversary as an accountant, Grandpa Alvin wanted to take advantage of this incredible adventure. I was not aware of the amount of the trip and whether I could afford it. He advised me that he would take care of the whole affair except amenities.

# Chapter 2:
# Grandpa Prepares Us For Travel

According to Grandpa, the travel agent at the agency told us we would have an adventurous time, and I could still accompany Grandpa regardless of my age.

My mom (Alice) and my dad (Allen) allowed me to go on the trip. They said it was all right if I was not alone if I was with Grandpa Alvin. I announced to all my friends that I was going on an adventure to Alaska. Amazingly, Grandpa was an avid traveler who had been to Alaska before.

Even though my friends were in awe and amazed by me because I was going on this adventurous trip to Alaska, I was afraid to go on the All-American Cruise Line ship.

Grandpa said we absolutely need an allowance for extra accessories and apparel purchases of about $100.00 per day on the seven- day trip to Alaska. My mom and dad gave me an allowance of $700.00.

Amazed at my upcoming adventure, Aunt Agnes gave me considerable allowance of about $500.00. Apparently, I was not aware that it actually cost this much per day.

# Chapter 3:
# The Trip Begins

The trip began in Abbeville, Oklahoma, from my house to the airport. We approached the airport with the assistance of a cab driver. We arrived at the airport in the early afternoon, around 1:00 p.m., for our airplane flight to Seattle, Washington.

Before we could get on the airplane, we had to go through security, where you had to have an actual boarding pass, driver's license, and/or passport. We arrived at the gate, about to get on the plane. The gate agent addressed us by announcing on the intercom that we were ready to depart on our airplane. It was time to get on the airplane.

Since our seats were arranged, I did not want to argue about which seat I was about to sit in because I always like to sit in the aisle. Grandpa asked me if I was adamant about having a window or aisle seat on the airplane. I chose the aisle seat. Grandpa also told the airline stewardess that I was allergic to peanuts.

While on the airplane, I met another girl named Alice who had the same name as my mom. She was all right except I was annoyed at her kicking my aisle seat.

The captain on the plane got our attention and announced that the air traffic controller had cleared our airplane to go. I attempted to assess if my seat belt was attached correctly.

While on the airplane, I got nervous and suffered anxiety when we approached a higher altitude. Of course, I am an amateur at flying.

I noticed that we had an athlete who was sitting in the aisle seat across from us. Admittedly, my admiration for him was an aggravation for him.

# Chapter 4:
# The Amazing Architecture
# of the All-American Line Cruise Ship

On the first day of the cruise, we arrived in the afternoon. Being awfully tired from traveling, we arrived at the ship. Apparently, my tiredness was catching up to me. I was in awe at the cruise ship's amazing appearance as it stood tall in the air.

The architecture of the cruise ship appealed to me. It appeared you could go anywhere on the ship because it was huge. While I was adamant and anxious about having the captain arrange a tour, the captain approved for us to go around the ship with the captain's assistant since the captain was not available. Agitated that the captain was not available, Grandpa told me we must adapt while not being angry.

Our assigned room was A-102. I was in awe of the amazing suite, which had a balcony with a table and many chairs outside. We liked the attention to detail and atmosphere of the cabin. Also, Grandpa and I approved of the large, ample room with beds.

# Chapter 5:
# The Amazing, Abundant,
# and Appetizing Food

Our cabin had apples, apricots, asparagus, avocados, almonds, and a bowl of ambrosia sitting on the table on an arranged tray. I was annoyed at having the asparagus amongst the arranged food put there by our cabin steward.

I asked the cabin steward if there was any more ambrosia, since we automatically ate all that was available on the arrangement. Apparently, Grandpa does not like avocados.

On my first night on the ship, I had such an appetite that I could not wait to even eat an apple, but I knew there was more to appreciate on the buffet. While at the table, I was acting up by putting my arm underneath my armpit and making noises. Grandpa said he did not approve of this action.

Apparently, anyone with an appetite will not go hungry since the cruise ship appears to have anything you want to eat. You can eat almost anywhere around the ship. I am even allowed to take advantage of eating an apple tart for dessert if I want to.

They actually have a lot of desserts that I could afford to eat because of my appetite, so I am going to have an additional piece. Grandpa was aware of the abundance of food but did not approve of me trying to eat everything available. So, I abandoned the idea and apologized for overeating.

After a long day and night, I could not wait to fall asleep, but I was absolutely enjoying the atmosphere of the cruise ship. I was anxiously awaiting the following day's activities.

# Chapter 6:
# Admiring Grandpa

I have always admired my grandfather, who was born in Anton, Alabama, on a small farm with many animals. His mother was Abigail, and his father was Alton.

I found out he was adopted when he was seven by another couple. This was an alarming announcement. He said it was a long time ago, not wanting to admit it.

Grandpa got angry, while also appearing to have anxiety, as he was talking about it. He was afraid to talk about it anymore because it would bring anguish.

I abandoned the idea of further action on the subject, so my ambition was to actually focus next on the many amazing, adventurous Alaskan activities to come.

# Chapter 7:
# The Sighting

The next day, I was hardly awake when Grandpa alerted me to a whale on the ship's side. It was awful in history that whales were hunted. I also saw an albatross fly over by our balcony.

Now, we are on to some amazing ports like Ketchikan, Juneau, and Seward. It is an awesome experience to see the trees' leaves in their Autumn best.

Also, there are plenty of animals to see near the trees, like moose and deer. The greatest attraction is seeing the amount of salmon swimming up a stream. I am aware and in complete awe of the beauty all around me.

I asked Grandpa if we could move to Alaska. My parents would never arrange or approve of this, but the idea sounded absolutely amazing.

# Chapter 8:
# Meeting an Author and Artist

While on board, I get to meet a male author and a female artist. I can only imagine how Alaska is  such a great area in which they can conduct their art. I wish I were as artistic as the artist and author.

Sometimes, I feel ashamed that I do not have this kind of ability. Being overly ambitious, my attraction to the craft of being an author or artist will help me decide to attain the necessary academic courses to further my craft. I might even allow myself to become an actor someday.

I was afraid to ask them anything because I am only a child, but I wanted to ask. The artist had her associate with her, which made it almost impossible to approach her to ask a question. In some ways, she is arrogant.

From the appealing brochure, I found out the artist also had an Associate Degree in Art, but I was not aware of what that meant. I just assumed that she is attracted to being an artist.

# Chapter 9:
# The Mishaps

I approached a dog sled during one of the activities off the ship. I apparently had an accident when I fell down and across the sled with an Alaskan Malamute attached to it.

Amazingly, the Alaskan Malamute was not aggressive, which I really appreciated. I must admit that my arm was aching. While not appearing agitated, I was embarrassed when the audience around me thought it was awful that I was injured. I am not a fan of attention.

While walking away from the Alaskan Malamute, an angry brown grizzly bear appeared from the forest. He averaged about seven foot tall with amazingly large claws and an angry face.

Our group of cruise ship adventurers was not aware of the amount of bears in this area. So, we analyzed the situation and approached an automobile coming down the road to alert the authorities and take us away from the area.

I admit I would like to see and be in awe of a bear. Accordingly, I would not want to be alone or aim to be near an aggressive bear who would eat you alive. Did I say aggressive?

While always being an adventurous girl, I would be afraid to anger the bear. My advice is to always be aware of the area around you. Bears usually are not affectionate, and you should not be affectionate to the animal.

In addition, I would not announce your arrival to the bear. Also, I would not want to get acquainted with or arrange a special visit with a bear that is aggravated.

# Chapter 10:
# The Amazing But Also Sad Day

It was an amazing day, but it was time to adjourn the activities. I had actually been too active today. Before getting into the automobile safely, I was tired, and my ankle was hurting from all the walking. We were able to safely get away from the aggressive bear.

When we returned to the ship, the doctor checked my aching arm and ankle. He put my arm in a sling. He also told me to take an aspirin to help with the pain in my arm and ankle.

## Chapter 11:
## The Adventure Ceases For Now

We arrived in port ahead of schedule. I was astonished that the adventure was about to approach an end. Grandpa asked the front desk to arrange for a taxi from the cruise ship to the airport. We were awaiting the announcement from the captain's assistant to disembark the ship.

Grandpa and I were amazed at how fast the taxi approached us when we left the ship. Next, we were whisked away to the airport.

Arriving at the airport in the taxi that we arranged at the port, I admitted to Grandpa that I was not ready for this adventure to be over. It was time to say goodbye to Alaska, while I waved aggressively from the airplane.

When Grandpa Alvin and I arrived at the airport in Oklahoma, my parents were awaiting our arrival on the airplane flight from Seattle, Washington.

No longer an amateur, I announced to Grandpa that I would like to go on another adventure with him, hopefully to Alaska again. As I appealed to Grandpa, I advised him not to take anyone else but me when he was ready to go away again. It was time to say goodbye to Grandpa.

# Chapter 12:
# Have You Been or Will You Go
# on An Adventure?

Have you ever been on an adventure? Use the travel log to write down places visited or places to visit.

Be sure to write down how you will get there. Will you go by car; bus; train; boat; cruise ship; plane; subway; walk; or a combination of some types of travel?

# TRAVEL LOG

**BUS-CAR-TRAIN-PLANE-WALK-BOAT-SUBWAY-CRUISE SHIP**

| PLACES VISITED | TYPE OF TRAVEL | PLACES TO VISIT | TYPE OF TRAVEL |
|---|---|---|---|
| 1. | | | |
| 2. | | | |
| 3. | | | |
| 4. | | | |
| 5. | | | |
| 6. | | | |
| 7. | | | |
| 8. | | | |
| 9. | | | |
| 10. | | | |

# Chapter 13:
# Tell Others About Your Adventure

FEW IDEAS:

1. Go to the library to research your trip location(s).

2. Write a travel journal.

3. Take pictures and post them in a special travel photo album.

4. Present a book report for your class.

5. Make a shadow box of your travel location.

6. Write a paragraph about your old trip or your new trip.

7. Watch a travel show that has your location on the show.

8. Ask an older person in your family about places he/she has visited.

9. Ask a travel agent about a place you want to visit.

10. Ask your classmate or friend about the place he / she has /will travel to.

11. Find travel brochures from the state rest stops or tourist welcome centers.

12. Ask a military person if he / she has traveled to a trip location.

13. Search the Internet with your parents' help for places you would like to go.

14. Write a list of 10 places you want to go in the United States.

15. List 10 countries you want to travel to someday.

16. Make a poster board of the locations you want to visit or have visited.

# Mark McCraw

I am a former Elementary School Teacher, Air Force and Air Force Reserve Military Member, Adjunct Professor, Daycare Teacher, Migrant Head Start Teacher, Corrections Officer, Pastor, and Non-Profit Executive. I have an Associate's Degree in Criminal Justice, a Bachelor's Degree in Theology, a Master's Degree in Elementary Education, a Master's Degree in Curriculum and Instruction, and two years of doctoral courses. This is my twelfth published book with more to come.

Currently, I am a member of the Society of Children's Book Writers and Illustrators (S.C.B.W.I.), Oklahoma Literacy Association (O.L.A.), and Oklahoma Writers Federation, Inc. (O.W.F.I.). Oklahoma Commissioner for the Scottish family MacRae's, Korea Defense Veterans Association (K.D.V.A.) Member, American Legion Member, Boy's State Recruiter in Oklahoma for my post, and Disabled American Veterans (D.A.V.) member and officer serving three terms as a Jr. Vice Commander.

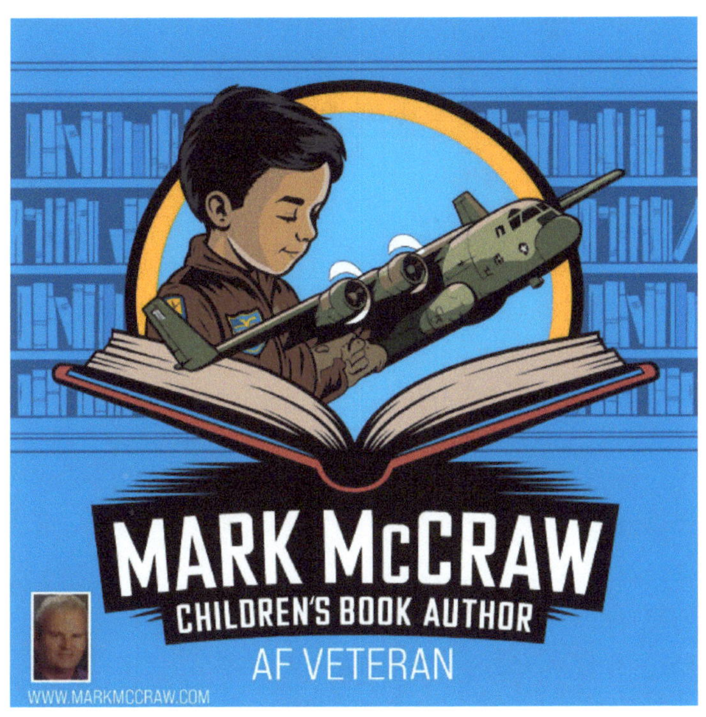


<u>MY OTHER BOOKS ARE AVAILABLE ON:</u>

www.markmccraw.com
www.amazon.com
www.barnesandnoble.com
www.walmart.com
www.booksamillion.com
www.bookshop.org
www.patriotwrites.com
www.authorsalcove.com
www.thriftbooks.com
www.archwaypublishing.com Did You Come Home for Lunch? (My first book)

<u>OTHER AMAZON WEBSITES:</u>

amazon.au (Australia)
amazon.br (Brazil)
amazon.ca  (Canada)
amazon.fr  (France)
amazon.de (Germany)
amazon.in (India)
amazon.it  (Italy)
amazon.jp  (Japan)
amazon.mx (Mexico)
amazon.es (Spain)
amazon.uk (United Kingdom)

<u>SOME OF MY OTHER BOOKS IN E-BOOKS:</u>

Amazon Apple
Baker and Taylor
Barnes and Noble
Borrow Box
Cloud Library
Everand
Fable
Find Away Voices
Gardners
Hoopla
Libby
Odilo
Overdrive
Palace Marketplace
Rakuten Kobo
Smashwords
Tolino
Vivlio

<u>AUDIBLES, KINDLES, HARDCOVER, AND SOFTCOVER</u>
Some books are listed as Audibles, Kindles, softcovers, and hardcovers. Please visit www.amazon.com for more details.

<u>LIBRARIES:</u>

<u>Florida Libraries</u>
Okaloosa County Library-
https://readokaloosa.org/

Santa Rosa County Library-
https://www.santarosa.fl.gov/975/Library- System

<u>Oklahoma Library</u>
Metropolitan Library System-
www.metrolibrary.org

# OUT OF THE UNITED STATES:

Check my website (www.markmccraw.com) for countries where books are distributed.
This list is not all-inclusive. Please check back periodically for updates.

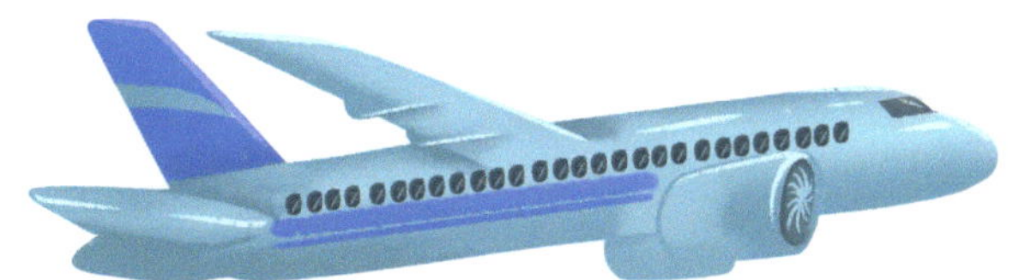